Something New for Rosh Hashanah

To GrandmaLis and Mabs—J.Y.

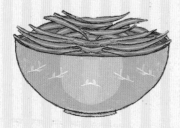

KAR-BEN PUBLISHING®
An imprint of Lerner Publishing Group, Inc.
241 First Avenue North
Minneapolis, MN 55401 USA

Website address: www.karben.com

Main body text set in Mikado.
Typeface provided by HVD Fonts.

Library of Congress Cataloging-in-Publication Data

Names: Yolen, Jane, author. | Battuz, Christine, illustrator.
Title: Something new for Rosh Hashanah / by Jane Yolen ; illustrations by Christine Battuz.
Description: Minneapolis, MN : Kar-Ben Publishing, [2021] | Audience: Ages 5–10. | Audience: Grades 2–3. |
    Summary: Five year-old Becca refuses to try any new foods, until her family persuades her that Rosh
    Hashanah, the Jewish New Year, is the perfect time to try something new.
Identifiers: LCCN 2020040837 (print) | LCCN 2020040838 (ebook) | ISBN 9781728403397 (lib. bdg.) |
    ISBN 9781728403403 (paperback) | ISBN 9781728428970 (ebook)
Subjects: CYAC: Stories in rhyme. | Rosh ha-Shanah—Fiction.
Classification: LCC PZ8.3.Y76 So 2021 (print) | LCC PZ8.3.Y76 (ebook) | DDC [E]—dc23

LC record available at https://lccn.loc.gov/2020040837

Manufactured in China
1-52107-50574-1/4/2022

0822/B1893/A3

Something New for Rosh Hashanah

Jane Yolen

illustrated by Christine Battuz

KAR-BEN
PUBLISHING

Becca doesn't like to eat,
like to eat, like to eat
anything that tastes like meat.
Or anything that's new.

"NO!" says Becca, "NO!"

Becca doesn't ever wish,
ever wish, ever wish
to eat a plate of smelly fish.
Or anything that's new.

Becca doesn't eat things green,
never green, ever green.
Not a lettuce leaf or bean.
Especially if they're new.

"ICK!" says Becca. "ICK!"

"Rosh Hashanah starts tonight,"
Mama says with great delight.
"Perhaps tonight you'd like to risk it
with a taste of Bubbe's brisket?"

Something new?

Papa answers in a flash,
in a dash, in a flash.
"I will shave off my mustache.
I'm tired of it now."

"NO!" says Becca, "NO!
I like the way it tickles."

Something new?

Mama says, "I'll learn to knit,
learn to knit, and knot and knit
nice warm sweaters that can fit
Aunt Jane or Cousin Al."

"Can I have one too?" asks Becca.

After shul, at Bubbe's house,
at Bubbe's table, Bubbe's house,
Becca, quiet as a mouse,
turns down chicken soup.

No to kugel, honey cake,
sweet honey cake, no honey cake.
Such a fuss does Becca make.
But wait! Here's something new!

Becca shouts:

"LOOK! LOOK AT ME!"

On her plate, one big green bean,
big green bean, big green bean.
The biggest green bean ever seen.
Becca eats it up.

And asks for another!

"And next year my New Year's wish,
New Year's wish, New Year's wish
will be to try gefilte fish!"
And everyone shouts, "YES!"

Full of NEWNESS, Becca grins.

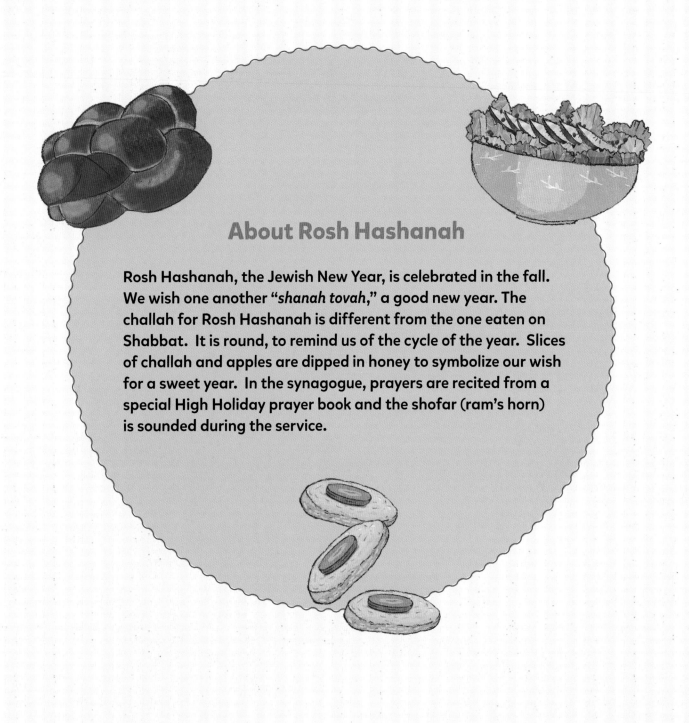

About Rosh Hashanah

Rosh Hashanah, the Jewish New Year, is celebrated in the fall. We wish one another "*shanah tovah*," a good new year. The challah for Rosh Hashanah is different from the one eaten on Shabbat. It is round, to remind us of the cycle of the year. Slices of challah and apples are dipped in honey to symbolize our wish for a sweet year. In the synagogue, prayers are recited from a special High Holiday prayer book and the shofar (ram's horn) is sounded during the service.

About the Author
Jane Yolen lives in Massachusetts and has written almost 400 books across all genres and age ranges, including the Bible story *Miriam at the River*. She has been called the Hans Christian Andersen of America and a contemporary Aesop.

About the Illustrator
Christine Battuz was born in France. She received her masters of fine arts at the Academy of Fine Arts of Perugia, Italy. A good friend convinced her that she was an illustrator; this wonderful friend became her husband. She has illustrated over 60 children's books. She lives in Quebec, Canada.